W9-CKW-570

SEYMOURINA

THE BOBBS-MERRILL COMPANY, INC.

INDIANAPOLIS   NEW YORK

SEYMOURINA

BY LAURENCE

THE BOBBS-MERRILL COMPANY, INC.
A SUBSIDIARY OF HOWARD W. SAMS & CO., INC.
PUBLISHERS   INDIANAPOLIS   KANSAS CITY   NEW YORK

To Seymourina

My name is Seymourina.
One day I fell asleep on the train.

When I opened my eyes, I was in a railway station full of people.

Alongside the train a farmer seemed to be waiting for me with a horsedrawn wagon filled with flowers.

"Excuse me, Sir, where am I?" I said.

"Little girl, you are in the Land of Love." Since I did not understand, the farmer said, "Come, let me show you around."

"See how many flowers grow here."

As we went on our way we met a country girl carrying a heavy load.
The farmer offered her a ride in his wagon.

Farther on, in the shadow of an apple tree in bloom, a teacher was telling his students a story:

"Once upon a time there was a little boy who tried to capture the sun and the stars. Because that is not possible, the boy was always sad.

"Why should anyone want to capture the treasures of heaven?" the teacher then asked.
"The sun and the stars shine for all of us."

Farther down the road we saw a soldier burying his arms in a field. "Now I can live in peace," he said.

Next we met a strange man.

He was trying to sing, but he howled.

He was trying to dance, but he fell.

He cried that no one loved him.

The farmer took him by the hand and comforted him.

The farmer then told us about a great scholar who had traveled as far as the moon looking for the Land of Love.

Just then we saw the scholar arriving on his rocket.

"I have found the Land of Love," he exclaimed.

"It is in my heart."

Then we met some musicians.
We followed them.

And all of us were happy on our ride together.